I AM EMPATH

HELPING KIDS UNDERSTAND EMPATHY

Copyright 2019 Amanda Marie Cottrell.
All rights reserved.
Library of Congress Cataloging-in-Publication Data
Available

ISBN: 9781689785235
Published by Art Mindfulness and Creativity
www.artmindfulnessandcreativity.com

Dedicated to all of the sensitive souls out there who feel so deeply. Also for my daughter Ella.

I am empathetic

Em-pa...
what?

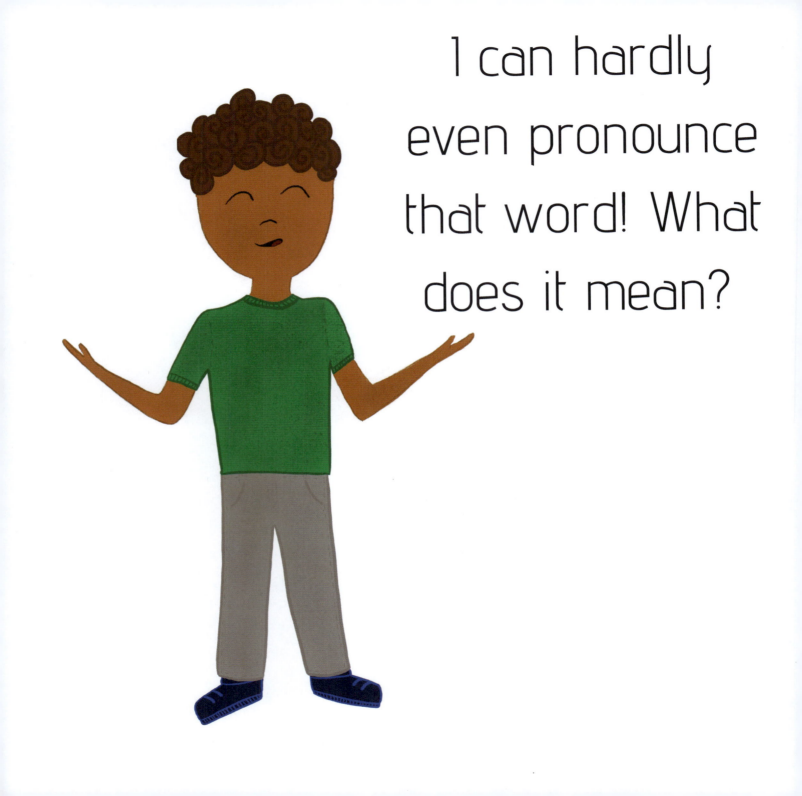

Well ... The dictionary defines it as, "showing an ability to understand and share the feelings of another."

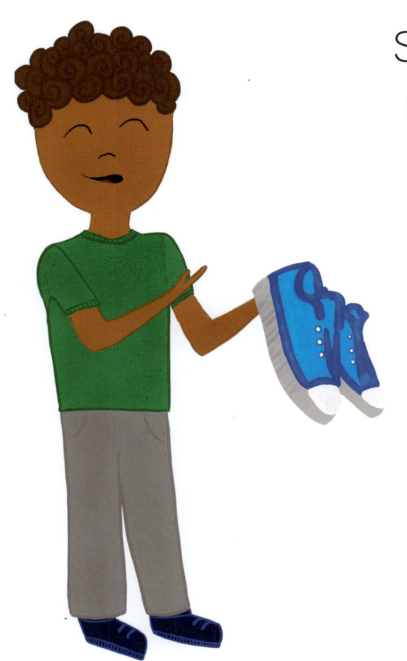

So empathetic means when you try to understand how another is feeling? Like the saying put yourself in their shoes?

Yes! Exactly

Am I empathetic when I help someone who is hurt and try to understand how they might be feeling?

What about when I try to understand how another person is feeling? Like when I show I care, even when I have never been in a situation like that.

You have it! Empathy can be showing kindness even when you do not totally understand what the other person is going through.

What about when I support someone who is trying something new?

Giving encouragement and supporting people has the spirit of empathy written all over it! Especially when you acknowledge the fear behind trying something new.

You can also show empathy when you hold space for someone by just listening.

Really!
I can be a
good listener.

Can I show empathy for animals, plants and the planet?

Absolutely! Empathy is about showing you care about feelings. I know my pets can feel. I am sure plants and the planet can too!

Sometimes showing empathy can be as simple as giving a hug or sending a caring note. Learning about different people and places through gaining an understanding and appreciation of their culture is another way to show empathy.

Wow! I never realized you could show empathy in so many ways!

If you are a very empathetic person sometimes people can take advantage of your kindness. So it is important to set clear boundaries for yourself.

Boundaries just ensure you are healthy first so that you can in turn help others!

Just as you cannot offer water to someone from an empty cup. You cannot truly help others if your energy has been depleted and you have nothing to give.

Empathy helps us understand other people and view the world through the lens of kindness and compassion.

TEACHING IDEAS:

Writing Prompts:

1. Think about a time when you noticed someone needed help. Take a few moments to remember all of the details of the situation. What it must have felt like to be the person who needed help. Write about the situation and the feelings that came up.

Art Projects:

1. Trace everyone in the classes hand and cut it out. Then go to each persons desk and write something caring about them.
2. Create kindness rocks to give to someone when the time is right.

Acting:

1. Brainstorm situations where someone could use their empathy skills. Plan out a play to explain the situation and what that characters might think, feel, do and say.

Believe, Create, Inspire

Amanda's mission is to help people develop and explore their creative gifts through art, yoga and mindfulness. She is an author, illustrator and teacher (B.A., B.Ed.,M.Ed) Amanda lives in Calgary, Alberta with her daughter Ella.

www.artmindfulnessandcreativity.com

Printed in Great Britain
by Amazon